The Legend of the Loon

By Kathy-jo Wargin
Illustrated by Gijsbert van Frankenhuyzen

Sleeping Bear Press

Dedicated to all grandmothers,
whose wisdom enriches our lives.

Text copyright © 2000 Kathy-jo Wargin
Illustration copyright © 2000 Gijsbert van Frankenhuyzen

Sleeping Bear Press
310 North Main Street, Suite 300
Chelsea, MI 48118
www.sleepingbearpress.com

Sleeping Bear Press is an imprint of The Gale Group, Inc.,
a division of Thomson Learning, Inc.

Printed and bound in Canada.

10 9 8 7 6 5 4 3 (case)
10 9 8 7 6 5 4 3 2 1 (pbk)

Library of Congress Cataloging-in Publication Data
Wargin, Kathy-jo.
The legend of the loon / by Kathy-jo Wargin;
illustrations by Gijsbert van Frankenhuyzen.
p. cm.
Summary: After being shown the wonders of nature by
Grandmother Lom, two children venture out on her boat alone,
find themselves in danger, and are rescued by a mysterious bird.
ISBN 1-886947-97-X (case) — ISBN 1-58536-167-4 (pbk)
[1. Grandmothers—Fiction. 2. Loons—Fiction.]
I. Frankenhuyzen, Gijsbert van, ill. II. Title.

PZ7.W234 Lg. 2000
[E]   00-025960

About The Legend of the Loon

For many centuries, the call of the loon has inspired and captivated people from many lands. In our story, we discover the magic of the Common Loon, *Gavia immer*. The species name *immer* is a derivative of the Scandinavian word *emmer*, which means blackened ashes, perhaps referring to the bird's dark mysterious plumage. The word loon is a derivative of the Scandinavian word *lom*, which means to walk in an odd or clumsy way, which possibly refers to the awkward way in which a loon attempts walking on land.

There are many legends of the loon, and they appear in many cultures. In my version, I used symbolism from the Scandinavian culture and its fairy tales to reconstruct some of the very first beliefs about this magnificent bird. In this tale, Grandmother Lom shows us that the grandmothers of a thousand years live in us, and we live in them.

We hope you enjoy this legend, and may the sound of the loon across great northern lakes always remind you of a great and magical love, where the echoes of the ones we love the most carry on across the water forever.

Kathy-jo Wargin

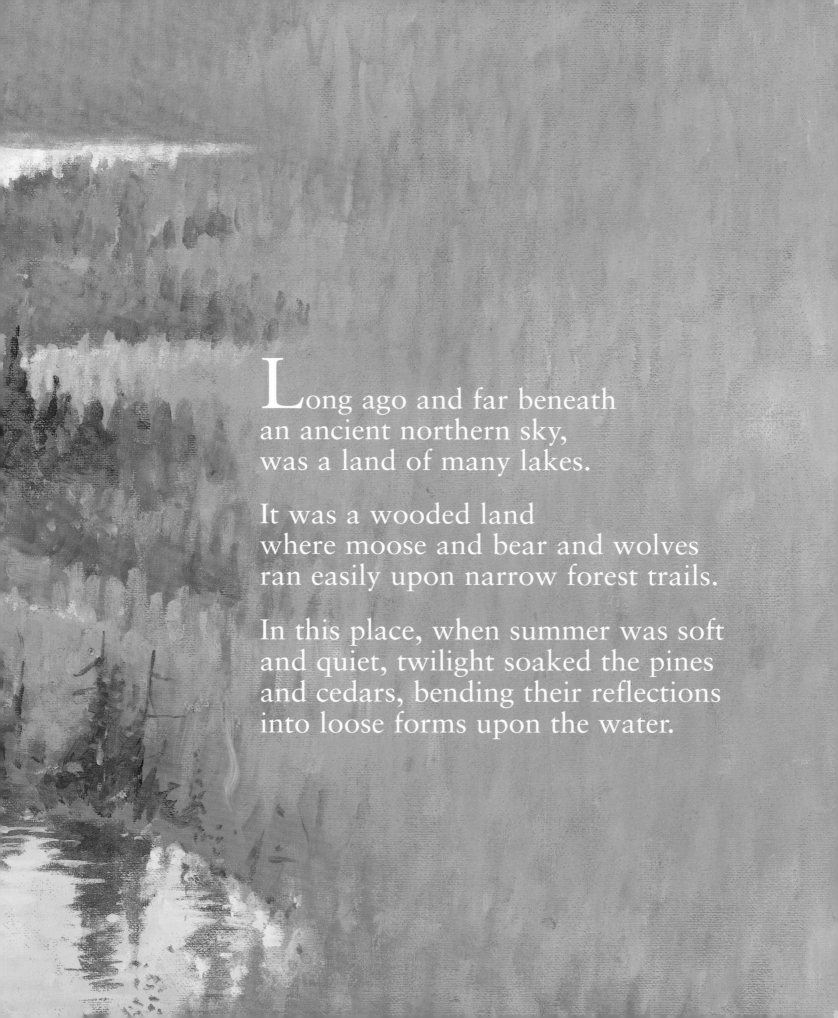

Long ago and far beneath
an ancient northern sky,
was a land of many lakes.

It was a wooded land
where moose and bear and wolves
ran easily upon narrow forest trails.

In this place, when summer was soft
and quiet, twilight soaked the pines
and cedars, bending their reflections
into loose forms upon the water.

In autumn, the forest became a wild feast of color
and sound. The sky filled with geese as they flew
beneath the approaching night, a hint of moonlight

In winter, it was a land
of frost and mist.
Every tree stood
silent beneath
a cover of snow,

only to become green
and awake again in the spring
when the forest floor was
a garden of lady's slippers
and ferns and newborn fawns.

In this land of water and wood was a sky-blue lake lined with stone cliffs. At the northern edge of the lake was a small bay shaped like a kettle, and tucked in its corner was a tiny village with cottages that were simple and square and brown.

Most of them sat side by side in two lazy rows not far from the lake.

There was one cottage, however, that sat apart from the others. It rested at the edge of the water near cattails and yellow water-lilies, and in it lived a very old woman who walked in an odd and clumsy way.

Her name was Grandmother Lom.

Grandmother Lom had lived in the northern woods as long as anyone in the village could remember. Her hair was as white as a cloud and her eyes seemed to laugh out loud.

Grandmother Lom had two grandchildren who lived in a cottage not far from her. They loved her very much and they visited her every day.

Every morning, the three of them walked through the forest picking blueberries and raspberries. The old woman was very slow and awkward, but she knew every trail and path by heart.

As they walked, Grandmother Lom taught them how to discover marvelous faces in the knots and cracks and shadows of white birch and jack pine trees. She said finding faces in trees makes you believe that everything in the forest is alive and watching you.

And when the sun was high and warm,
they would all hold hands and dance
around in a circle. Grandmother Lom said
the wind in the aspen trees and the sound
of sparrows was the music of nature.
The children agreed.

But there was one thing the children
loved to do more than anything else,
and that was to ride with Grandmother
Lom in her old white boat.

She always rowed slowly so the children could dip their fingertips into the ripples, where the moving water felt silky, like the wings of a new moth.

When they reached the edge of the shallow bay, which was as far as Grandmother Lom said was safe to go, she would plop her hand into the water and scoop up sunfish or walleye for dinner.

The children thought Grandmother Lom was magic.

Most often they returned home just as the sky was dimming and crickets were chirping. Grandmother Lom would place large stones in a circle at the water's edge and build a fire out of sticks and logs, so they could warm themselves. On one such night the children sat close to her and asked many questions:

"Where did you come from, Grandmother Lom?"
The old woman smiled and said in a whisper—

"I am the daughter of the Lakes,
Lakes, the daughter of Woods,
Woods, the daughter of Wilderness,
And Wilderness, the daughter of Song."

The children looked very serious,
like they didn't understand,
so Grandmother Lom went on
to explain—"My little ones, that means
the grandmothers of a thousand years
live in us, and we live in them.
They are the spirit of the wilderness,
and it is their love and strength we
carry in our dream-soul."

The children leaned closer.

"Dream-soul? What is a dream-soul?" they asked.

"Ah, little ones," she said, "your dream-soul is the very center of your heart, where all of the things you believe in and wish for come together like earth and water and sky. It is where all of the beautiful things you love stay forever and ever."

With that, the children drew even closer to her side.

"What does our dream-soul look like, Grandmother Lom?"

"Imagine a soft white mist rolling over a shining silver lake on a day when the woods are still because there is no wind and no sound. In the center of that mist is one bright place where the sun shines down upon the water. The lake, the mist, and the place of light is what your dream-soul looks like, my little ones."

And then the children grew very curious.

"Does everyone have a dream-soul?" they asked.

"Yes, we all have a dream-soul, but we all carry something different in it."

"Grandmother Lom, what do you carry in your dream-soul?"

"Ah, my little ones,
My dream-soul carries all of the things I love, like
the sound of white birch trees rattling in the wind,
the scent of balsam fir on a crisp morning,

and the exact moment when the blue of the lake meets the first gold of night. And it carries you, my little ones, most of all it carries you."

As Grandmother Lom spoke, the embers from the fire pulsed from orange to black to white. The light of a thousand stars fell upon the water while northern lights danced back and forth in the sky, setting the lake aglow. The children noticed Grandmother Lom's reflection upon the water. She looked as if she was wearing the night and the stars on her back, the northern lights as a beautiful necklace, and a kindled flame in her eyes. The children thought she looked beautiful, and they felt warm in her love, knowing they were the very best part of her dream-soul. At that moment, they felt Grandmother Lom in their dream-soul, too.

One day, the grandchildren went to the shore without Grandmother Lom and stepped into the small white boat.

They rowed across the shallow bay, where perch and minnows darted beneath ripples of water.

They laughed. They sang.

They rowed a bit here and there, and did not notice how they drifted far beyond the comfort of the shallow bay.

And then everything got quiet.

The lake was smooth like glass, and sweeps of white
and gray mist seemed to pour up from the water.
It became fuller and fuller, and thicker, and higher.

Soon, they could not see the water.
They could not see the land.
They could barely see each other.

They were very frightened, so they began to cry.

On shore, Grandmother Lom heard their cries and knew that something was terribly wrong.

The old woman hobbled to the lake and stepped in as far as she could go, and began to wave her arms back and forth. She pressed her face to the sky and sang out in a wild sad cry:

"Where are you?
Where are you?

Where are yooooou?" She sang out.

Grandmother Lom waved her arms back and forth in the fog. As she did, her cry grew louder and louder, and her words ran close together in a very strange way.

"Where are yoooooooooooou?" she called.

Grandmother Lom kept crying out and waving her arms back and forth, back and forth. Her body was shivering and her eyes were moist with tears. Her voice echoed with tremendous love and worry for her grandchildren.

"Where are yooooooooou?" She cried.

The sound rang out across the water. It was wild and strange and sad. Every tree shivered, every red fox and mink and marten stood motionless at the water's edge.

It drew all of the people from the village.

The grandchildren heard it and knew that it was Grandmother Lom calling them to shore. They tried to row toward her voice, knowing it would take them back into the shelter of the bay. The fog was very thick so the children listened very carefully.

And then suddenly, it stopped.

The children gasped, afraid they would be lost
forever. And just then, silence pierced the air and
sunlight broke through a small opening in the fog.
In one swift motion, a beautiful bird swept over-
head. The children had never seen such a creature
before, yet it seemed familiar. Its eyes were red
like firelight and its body was the color of
blackened ashes. On its back were a
thousand stars and it wore
a necklace of the
northern lights.

The bird let out a wild beautiful cry and then
circled the boat as if to say, follow me, follow me.

The children followed the bird through the mist.
They rowed and rowed as it led them away from
the cliffs and into the shelter of the bay. As they
neared the shore, the bird looked back at them for
one moment and then disappeared into the fog.

With the boat safely on shore, the children
looked around for Grandmother Lom.

But she was not there.

The children saw the white apron she wore every day
lying wet and wrinkled in the sand.

At that moment, as the children thought
Grandmother Lom was gone,
a long, rich sound echoed through the air.

It sailed across the water and deep into the center
of every living creature and person of the forest.

Like magic, it came from the wonderful
creature who had saved their lives.

It came from Grandmother Lom.

And there she was in the mist, a dark gentle bird floating softly upon the water while birch trees rattled in the wind and the air smelled of balsam fir. Everyone listened to her song with great joy in their hearts, because Grandmother Lom was calling out to the grandchildren she loved so much, letting them know they will be part of her dream-soul forever.

And always, her song remains the sound of a wonderful and magical love, the echo of our dream-souls, where all that we wish for, all that we believe in, and all that we love is able to stay forever and ever.

A Song for Grandmother Lom

Long ago and far away,
In a land of blue.
Where the woods are dark and deep
Damp with morning dew.

There lived a woman, some believe
very old and gray
She saved her children with a song
And then she flew away.

Now upon the northern lakes,
Her dream-soul echoes through—
In the beauty of her song

My little ones,
Where are you?
She sings
My little ones,
Where are you?

Kathy-jo Wargin

When author Kathy-jo Wargin was a young girl growing up on the Iron Range of Minnesota, she heard many old stories about the lakes and woods and animals that exist there. Many of them were legends that came from the colorful mix of cultures and people of that area. Always inspired by nature, it is her goal to show how beautiful and magical the most simple things in life can be. Her other stories include the award-winning legends *The Legend of Sleeping Bear* and *The Legend of Mackinac Island*, as well as *M is for Mitten* and *Michigan The Spirit of the Land*. She lives in northern Michigan where she likes to spend time walking through the beautiful woods and listening to the wonderful stories that exist there.

Gijsbert van Frankenhuyzen

From a very young age Gijsbert wanted to be an artist and children's book illustrator. His work can be seen in *The Blue Spruce*, written by former New York Governor Mario Cuomo, as well as *The Legend of Sleeping Bear* and *The Legend of Mackinac Island* with author Kathy-jo Wargin. As an artist, Gijsbert feels that illustrating children's books has given him the freedom to be very imaginative and to experiment with bold color combinations.

He travels throughout the country presenting programs to schoolchildren, sharing with them that sketching animals is as easy as drawing circles, squares and triangles. True to the philosophy his father taught him, Gijsbert encourages all children to follow their dreams and make their hobby their career, whatever it may be.

Gijsbert would like to give a BIG thanks to Nick and Katie Garrity for being the models for Grandmother Lom's grandchildren. They did a wonderful job and were fun to work with.